To our family twins, Kimberly and Amanda—
who are double fun!

—B. R.

To Bobby, for his love and support in my return
to my first love, children's books

—L. B. C.

Henry Holt and Company, LLC
Publishers since 1866
175 Fifth Avenue
New York, New York 10010
www.HenryHoltKids.com

Distributed in Canada by H. B. Fenn and Company Ltd.

Library of Congress Cataloging-in-Publication Data
Roberts, Bethany.
Double trouble Groundhog Day / by Bethany Roberts ; illustrated by Lorinda Bryan Cauley.—1st ed.
p. cm.
Summary: When Grampie Groundhog decides to retire from forecasting the weather,
he has twins Greta and Gregory draw straws to see who will take over the important job,
but the winner is so nervous the two put aside their squabbling and work together.
ISBN-13: 978-0-8050-8280-7 / ISBN-10: 0-8050-8280-8
[1. Woodchuck—Fiction. 2. Twins—Fiction. 3. Brothers and sisters—Fiction.
4. Cooperativeness—Fiction. 5. Groundhog Day—Fiction.] I. Cauley, Lorinda Bryan, ill. II. Title.
PZ7.R5396Dou 2008 [E]—dc22 2007040043

First Edition—2008 / Designed by Véronique Lefèvre Sweet
The artist used watercolor and colored pencil on Arches watercolor
paper to create the illustrations for this book.
Printed in China on acid-free paper. ∞

1 3 5 7 9 10 8 6 4 2

Double Trouble Groundhog Day

By Bethany Roberts

Illustrated by Lorinda Bryan Cauley

Henry Holt and Company ✦ New York

ONE FALL EVENING...
on Weathervane Mountain, the Groundhog family gathered in their burrow. They were enjoying one final filling feast before their long winter nap.

The twins, Gregory and Greta, squabbled over the last piece of pumpkin pie.

"I got it!" said Gregory.

"I got it first!" cried Greta.

Gregory poked Greta.

Greta bumped Gregory.

Gregory tweaked Greta's tail.

Greta pulled Gregory's ear.

"Twins!" said Dad Groundhog, shaking his head.

"Double trouble," said Grannie Groundhog with a smile.

"Late breaking news! Late breaking news!" Grampie Groundhog stood up and clinked his glass. "There's a change in the wind," he announced.

"As you know, every year, on the second day of February, I pop out of the ground. If I see my shadow, there will be six more weeks of winter. If I don't see my shadow, we'll spring into spring."

Gregory stopped poking Greta to listen.

Greta stopped bumping Gregory to listen.

"But I am getting old and a bit under the weather," said Grampie. "So I'm turning our family forecasting job over to one of you young 'uns."

The twins jumped up and down.

"I'll do it!" cried Gregory.

"No, I want to do it!" cried Greta.

"Me!" said Gregory.

"Me, me, me!" cried Greta.

"We will draw straws," said Grannie Groundhog. "The one with the longer straw gets the job."

Gregory pushed his glasses back on his nose. "I'll be in all the newspapers," he said.

"I'll be on TV," Greta said. She danced a happy star dance all around the room.

"Greta, you pick," said Grampie.

Greta stopped dancing, squeezed her eyes tight, and wished. Then she picked a straw.

"I get the job," crowed Gregory. "I'll be famous!"
He looked at himself in the mirror. "Gregory the Great!"

"Gregory the Gross," said Greta.
"Poor loser!" said Gregory.

Greta stuck out her tongue.

Gregory chased Greta with a pillow.

"Twins," said Mom Groundhog, shaking her head.

"Double trouble!" said Grampie with a wink.

"Time for bed," said Dad Groundhog. "The world is counting on you, Gregory!"

"You betcha," said Gregory, brushing his teeth. "Gregory the Great, World Famous Forecaster, preparing for bed."

Greta rolled her eyes.

Gregory set his alarm clock for February 2. Soon everyone was sound asleep, except Gregory.

"Let's see," he thought. "If I see my shadow, I say, 'Spring will come soon!' No, no, that's if I *don't* see my shadow. If I don't see my shadow, I say, 'It will be winter for six more weeks!' No, that's if I *see* my shadow . . ."

Gregory drifted off to sleep.

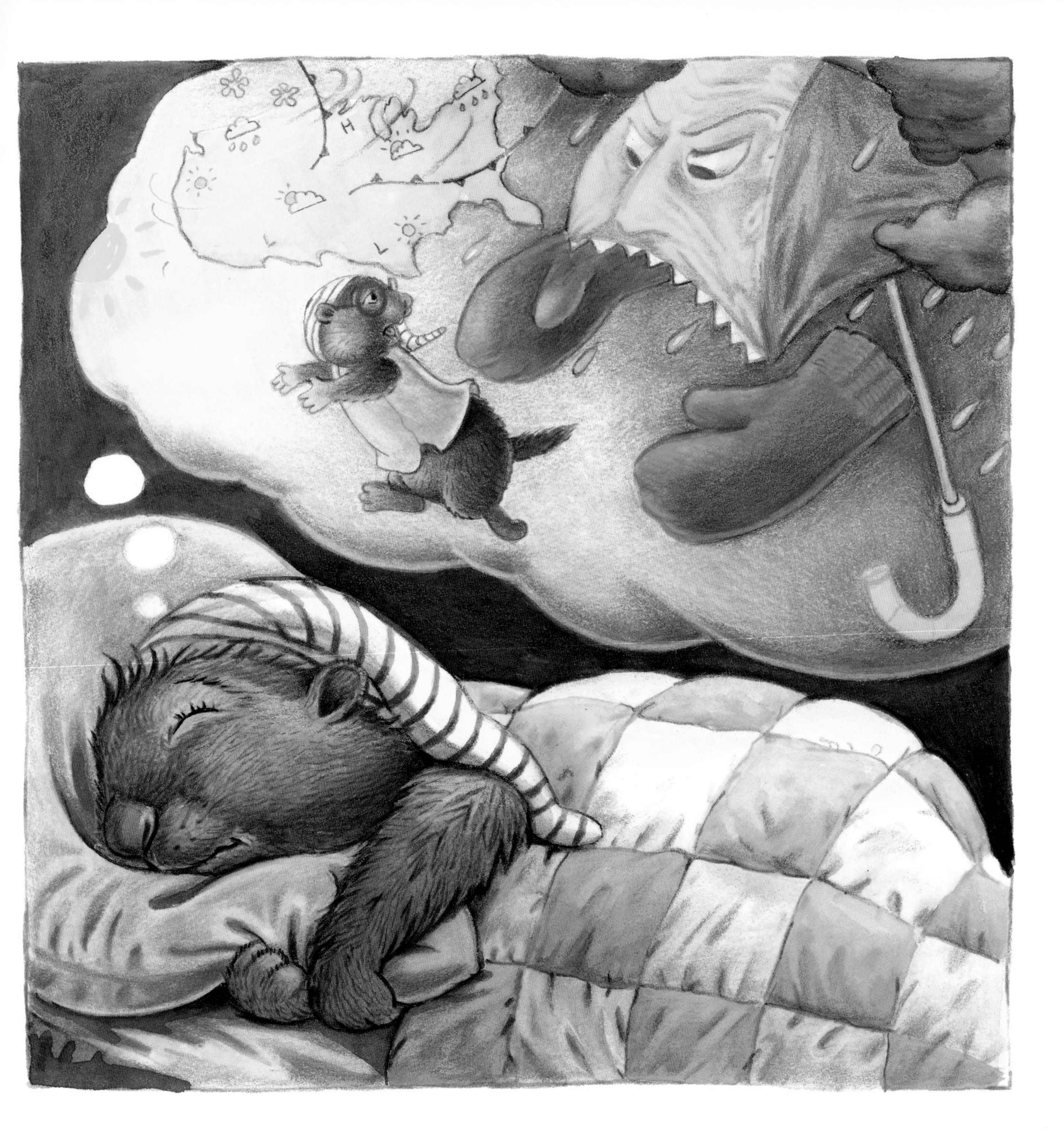

In his dreams, weather maps swirled, umbrellas had teeth, and giant mittens chased him.

Still sleeping, Gregory slowly got out of bed and popped out of the hole. He stood on a stump and waved his eyeglasses. “Six more shadows,” he shouted. “Winter is springing soon!”

Then he crawled back under his warm quilt, and fell into a deep sleep for the rest of the winter.

R-I-N-G! The alarm clock rang.

Greta woke up. It was February 2.

But Gregory was still sound asleep!

"Gregory, wake up," cried Greta. "You have to forecast the weather!"

Gregory moaned. "I'm sooooo tired."

Greta danced a wake-up dance around the room.
Gregory plopped his pillow over his eyes.

Greta tickled him.
Gregory pulled the covers over his head.

Greta blew a trumpet.
TROOOOT! TROOOOT! TROOOOT!
"Mmf," Gregory mumbled.

"If you don't get up," said Greta, "how will farmers know when to plant crops? How will fathers know if they need fishing rods or fireplace logs?

"How will mothers know if they should pack picnics or bake bread?

"And how will children know if they need umbrellas and kites or sleds and mittens?"

"Umbrellas with teeth," Gregory mumbled. "Giant mittens."

"Umbrellas don't have teeth, and mittens are small," said Greta. "You must have had a bad dream. Are you getting stage fright?"

"I'm a little nervous," admitted Gregory from under the covers.

Gregory rolled over and opened one eye. Then he opened the other eye. Everything was blurry.

"Where are my glasses?" he asked.

"Where did you put them?" asked Greta.

"I don't know. All I can remember is something about shadows," said Gregory.

They looked under
the quilt.

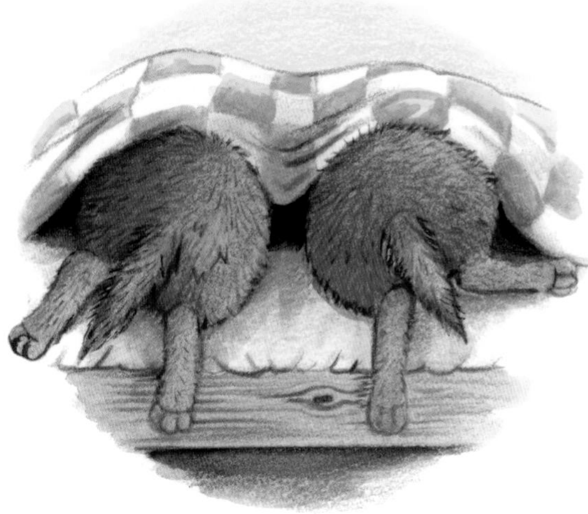

They looked inside
the dresser.

They looked in
his slippers.

They looked everywhere.
But Gregory's glasses could not be found.

"This gets worse and worse," moaned Gregory. "How can I see my shadow if I can't see my own paw in front of my face?"

"I'll help you," said Greta. "Hurry! The world is waiting!"

Greta grabbed Gregory, and together they scrambled out of the hole.

Lights flashed. Cameras whirred. Reporters scribbled.

"Am I seeing double?" asked Mayor Marva Moose.

"Hey, there are *two* groundhogs!" cried the TV crew.

"So what's your prediction?" asked Reporter Jack Rabbit.

"Tell us, tell us!" shouted the crowd.

"There is no shadow," Greta whispered into Gregory's ear.

Gregory's knees shook. He took a deep breath. "Th-there is n-no sh-shadow," he squeaked.

"SPRING WILL COME SOON!" added Greta.

"SPRING! HOORAY!" shouted the reporters.

"SPRING! HOORAY!" shouted the crowd.

"And here are your glasses, right on this stump. You must have been sleepwalking," said Greta.

SPRING!

Everyone waved Groundhog banners.
They held Groundhog balloons.
The band began to play the "Groundhog Stomp."
Everyone danced and sang.

SPRING!
Spring is coming SOON!

Later that day, the twins went to the newsstand. *The Groundhog Gazette* headlines read:

"NO TROUBLE! AND THAT'S DOUBLE!"

"But I'd have been in trouble without your help," said Gregory. "We make a great team."

"You betcha!" said Greta, hugging him.

Gregory waved the newspaper.

"I'll show this to Grampie," he said.

"No, I will, I will!" cried Greta.

Greta tweaked Gregory's tail.

Gregory pulled Greta's ear.

Greta chased Gregory down the hill, around a bush, and into the burrow.

"By thunder," said Grampie, squinting at the paper. "You two young 'uns sure are fine forecasters. Not a shadow of a doubt!"

Gregory pushed his glasses back on his nose.

"I can't wait 'til we can do it again next year," he said.

"We?" asked Greta.

"Of course!" said Gregory.

Greta grinned. "Make that double!"